First published in 1990 by
André Deutsch Limited
105-106 Great Russell Street, London WC1B 3LJ

British Library Cataloguing in Publication Data

Thomas, Iolette
Princess Janine.
I. Title   II. Northway, Jennifer, *1955-*
823' .914 [J]

ISBN 0 233 98421 6

Printed in Hong Kong

PRINCESS JANINE

Iolette Thomas

Illustrated by Jennifer Northway

ANDRE DEUTSCH

Janine yawned and stretched s–l–o–w–l–y, then opened her eyes. It was 7-o-clock and her sister Ama was still asleep.

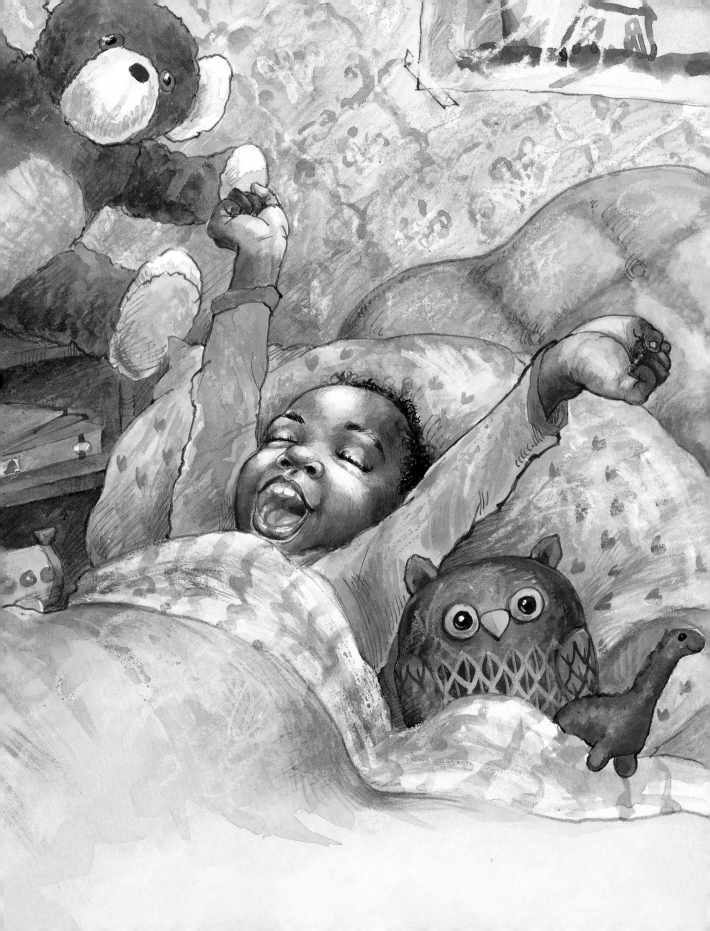

"It's too early to get up," she groaned, and turned over.
Suddenly, she was wide awake. She knew why she had woken up.
Today was the day they were going to the Safari Park. Yesterday,
Mum had made fried chicken, salt fish fritters and sweet potato
pudding while Janine was at play school, and they had bought crisps,
chocolate chip cookies, oranges, apples and a carton of fruit juice on
the way home. This morning, Janine and her father would make ham,
corned beef and cheese sandwiches while her mother filled a flask with
hot tomato soup. What a feast!

Janine jumped out of bed just as her mother came in.
"Well done, you're up," said her mother, "Go and brush your teeth quickly, then you can help Dad make the sandwiches, while I get Ama ready."

Janine was a good helper, and soon there was a big pile of sandwiches on the table, ready for packing into a large basket, along with everything else.

"Better have some breakfast," said her father, but Janine was much too excited. She ran upstairs and tied her ribbon, then popped a bar of chocolate into her dungarees pocket just in case . . . What else would she need? Oh yes, the camera her cousin Christopher had lent her. That went round her neck.

"When I grow up, I'm going to be a photographer," she told her
mother.
"That's nice, dear," said her mother absent-mindedly, wrapping
pieces of fruit cake in greaseproof paper.

At last they were ready and, when everything was packed into the car, they all climbed in. Janine's father started the engine and they were off.

At first, Janine found the journey very interesting.
She counted clocks, and spotted red cars.

But after a while she got thirsty. "Have a drink," said her mother and Janine did.

Then, when no one was looking she ate her bar of chocolate.

A little later she felt ill. "I don't feel well," she moaned.
"It's not like you to be travel sick," said her mother,
and Janine was too ashamed to tell her about the chocolate.

Luckily, just at that moment, her father said, "We'll stop here for ten minutes and stretch our legs."

Janine felt much better after a run in the fresh air, and enjoyed looking out of the car window again. She noticed a man painting his house, and said, "I've changed my mind about being a photographer; I'm going to be a painter when I grow up."

"Good," said her father. "Our house will certainly need a coat of paint by then."

Later, they all played a game of I–Spy. When it was their father's turn, he said, "I spy something beginning with S."

"A sparrow," said Janine.

"Wrong," said her father.

Janine guessed again. "Socks,"

"No – guess again, or do you give up?"

But this time Janine knew the answer. "Signs to the Safari Park," she shouted as they followed the arrows.

The lady who collected the entrance fee gave Janine's father a sticker that said, "We had a rip-roaring time at Chapton Safari Park."

"But we haven't even seen the animals yet," complained Janine.
"You will," said the lady. "Just follow the path. Have a nice day, now."

"Look, there are some monkeys," said their mother and, when Janine looked closely at the trees, she saw lots of monkeys on the branches. Some came close to the car and one, whose baby was hugging her waist, came right up to it.

"I must take some photographs," said Janine, and she clicked away while the monkeys posed.

They saw all sorts of different animals. Once, when they stopped the car a baby zebra came up and breathed on the window. Ama looked frightened.

"There's no need to be frightened," said Janine, and she showed Ama how brave she was by moving her hand up and down the glass.

When they drove on again they saw wolves, foxes, tigers and, finally, the lions. One of the lions stood in front of the car and looked at them for a long time before stalking majestically away.

"That was scary, wasn't it?" said their mother.

Father didn't seem to have heard. "I'm hungry after all this driving," he said.

"Me, too," agreed Janine, and they headed for the picnic area, which was crowded with tourists. Janine couldn't understand what some of them were saying, so she guessed they were people from all sorts of different countries.

"Eat up," said her mother. "We don't want to take any food home with us."

Janine did not need to be told twice – she tucked into the food and in next to no time most of the containers were nearly empty.

After lunch her mother said, "All this sitting around isn't good for me, so I'm going for a walk." Ama held out her hands to be lifted up. "I'm coming, too," said Janine, putting a juicy red apple in one pocket and some biscuits in the other – just in case she got hungry later. "I'll join you in a minute," said their father as Janine, Ama and their mother walked to the Kiddies Corner.

There was lots to see and do, but the best moment was when a baby elephant ambled over, put his trunk in Janine's pocket and pulled out her biscuits. Janine laughed, and stroked the elephant while he munched her emergency rations.

Ama, seeing Janine stroking him, put out her hand and gave him a pat. "Doggie," she said.

"I wish we could take him home," said Janine. "He wouldn't be any trouble."

The elephant's keeper heard her. "You can't do that," he said, laughing. "His mother would miss him. In fact, here comes his mother, now. Come to see that her baby is safe."

A large elephant lumbered over and pushed her trunk into Janine's pocket.

"Visitors mustn't feed the animals," said the keeper quickly, but he was too late; the elephant had already eaten Janine's juicy, red apple.

"Oh dear," said Janine, feeling guilty. "But I didn't feed her, she took it."
The keeper winked. "Never mind," he said. "Nellie likes an apple
every now and then and there's no harm done."
Nellie seemed to like Janine. She felt all over her with her long trunk,
then, as if she had decided there was no food left, reached up into the
branches of the nearest tree, pulled some leaves off and stuffed them
into Janine's pocket.

"Well, I never," said the keeper, "she's saying thank you for the apple. But I can think of a better way."
He turned to Janine's mother and whispered in her ear. Janine's mother smiled, glanced at Janine and nodded. The keeper took Nellie's trunk and pulled it gently towards Janine. Then, suddenly, Nellie wound her trunk around Janine's waist and lifted her into the air. Janine gasped, but before she had time to be really frightened, she was safely seated on the elephant's back – just as her father arrived with the camera.

"Look at me," shouted Janine, "Up here. I'm in the sky!"
One of the tourists who had been watching laughed. "You look just
like a princess," she said, and Janine smiled the widest of smiles,
because now she knew what she was going to be when she grew up.
"I'm going to be a princess," she told her father.
"Princess who?" asked her father.
"Princess Janine, of course," said Janine proudly.